STEVEN KROLL ANITA LOBEL
Looking for Daniela
A Romantic Adventure

HOLIDAY HOUSE/NEW YORK

Library of Congress Cataloging-in-Publication Data

Kroll, Steven.
Looking for Daniela.

Summary: Antonio, a street performer who admires
a rich merchant's daughter, must use his talents in
juggling, tightrope walking, and guitar playing when
he rescues her from bandits and tries to get her
home again.
[1. Robbers and outlaws—Fiction. 2. Adventure
and adventurers—Fiction. 3. Performing arts—
Fiction] I. Lobel, Anita, ill. II. Title.
PZ7.K9225Lk 1988   [E]   87-29071
ISBN 0-8234-0695-4

For Anita, who inspired it, with
thanks to Daniel Thomases
S.K.

For Leslie and Adam, with love
A.L.

Antonio and his dog Bruno lived in a small room at the Inn of the Three Kings in a village by the sea.

Each day Antonio went to the piazza to perform. He juggled apples and oranges. He tied his tightrope between two trees and walked across it. He did flips in the air and played his guitar.

The villagers loved watching Antonio. They laughed and clapped and threw coins into the hat Bruno carried.

Antonio had a special friend called Daniela. Her father was a rich merchant, and she lived in a very big house.

Each morning, she waved to Antonio from her window. "*Buon giorno*, Antonio," she called. Sometimes she slipped away and danced with him in the piazza.

One day, when Antonio looked up at the window, Daniela was not there. He knocked on her door.

A servant answered. Daniela's mother was weeping in the hallway.

"What has happened, dear lady?" Antonio asked.

"Bandits have kidnapped my daughter!" sobbed Daniela's mother. "They want our fortune, and they will show no mercy!"

Antonio ran to the piazza. Daniela was not there. He ran to the harbor. "Bandits have stolen the *Valentina*," said a captain, "and they have taken Daniela!"

Far away on the horizon,
Antonio saw the stolen ship.

He and Bruno borrowed a boat and sailed after it. They sailed and sailed. When they reached the next port, they saw the *Valentina* tied up at the dock. The ship was deserted. Just as Antonio and Bruno wondered what to do next, an old man stepped out of the shadows.

"They've taken your lady to the Inn of the Golden Eagle," he said. He pointed out the way, and Antonio and Bruno set off.

When they got to the inn, they spied the bandits drinking and shouting at a table by the fireplace.

"Saucy little girl, that Daniela!" said one.

"Good thing we locked the upstairs room!" shouted another.

Antonio sneaked out the back door. A candle was flickering in the upstairs window.

He threw his tightrope over a branch of a nearby tree and started climbing. As he was about to tap on the window, Daniela opened it.

"Antonio!" she cried.

"Shhh," he said, "I've come to rescue you."

Antonio and Daniela slid down the rope and dropped gently to the ground. As they landed, one of the bandits came outside and saw them.

"She's escaping!" he shouted. "Catch her!"

Daniela, Antonio, and Bruno ran. All the bandits ran after them.

At the edge of town, Antonio saw a wagon filled with hay.

"Let's hide!" he whispered.

He dove into the hay, and Daniela and Bruno followed. When the bandits reached the wagon, they ran right by.

A while later, Antonio poked his head out. No one was there. He and Daniela and Bruno jumped from the hay wagon and started to walk.

"Who goes there?" came a voice from the dark.

Antonio stopped short. "Two travelers chased by bandits," he said.

A shepherd stepped forward and smiled. "You've no reason to be afraid. I will hide you for the night."

There were many sheep in the field. There was a fire and food, and before Antonio knew it, his eyes were closing. The shepherd covered him and Daniela with blankets, and a sheep snuggled down by their heads to make a pillow.

In the morning, the shepherd gave them bread and milk. He asked no questions, wished them well, and sent them on their way.

When they had gone only a short distance, Daniela said, "Will we ever get home, Antonio?"

Antonio hugged her. "Of course," he said. "You must have faith."

They kept on walking. They were getting tired and dusty.

Suddenly a gleaming carriage pulled up beside them. A grand lady in furs and jewels opened the door.

"My name is Signora Canaletto," she said to Antonio. "You look like a performer. Would you like to appear at my theater?"

Antonio bowed. "Bandits are after us, dear lady. I cannot take time to perform."

"You will be safe with me," said Signora Canaletto. "Perform tonight, and I will help you."

Antonio, Daniela, and Bruno climbed into the carriage. It had soft leather seats. By the time Antonio and Daniela reached Signora Canaletto's villa, they had told her the whole story.

That night Antonio and Daniela appeared in disguise at the theater. They danced the way they did in the village piazza, and Antonio played a mandolin he had found backstage. As a final touch, Antonio juggled silver balls, and then he juggled bottles.

The audience clapped and shouted until they were hoarse. But Antonio and Daniela were worried. They knew the bandits might appear at any moment.

And they were right! Four bandits were creeping toward the stage!

Antonio and Daniela slipped away.
Backstage, Signora Canaletto pointed to an open door.
In the field behind the theater was a huge balloon.
"You will escape in this," said Signora Canaletto.
"My guards will protect you."
The basket wobbled slightly
as Antonio helped Daniela over the side.
He handed Bruno up to her and climbed in himself.

They were off, soaring away into the night sky. Antonio looked down. The bandits were thundering along on horses and waving their fists.

Antonio pulled a sandbag loose and hurled it at their heads. Then Signora Canaletto's guards galloped up. They charged the bandits and began to fight them, as a gust of wind picked up the balloon and carried it high above the treetops.

The balloon flew out over the ocean as the sun was rising. And then it floated down. Gently it landed in the village piazza.

Daniela's parents came running up.

"Antonio saved me!" cried Daniela.

"He must be rewarded," said her father.

And so he was. Daniela's father gave him a bag of gold and a beautiful new cape.

But for Antonio, the best part came the next day. As he
walked toward the piazza to perform, Daniela waved to him
from her window.